# BABY SHARK and FRIENDS
# TWINKLE, TWINKLE, YOU'RE A STAR!

Art by John John Bajet

Cartwheel Books
An Imprint of Scholastic Inc.
New York

ISBN 978-1-338-72936-8 • 10 9 8 7 6 5 4 3 2 1          21 22 23 24 25
First printing, May 2021 • Designed by Doan Buu
Scholastic Inc., 557 Broadway, New York NY 10012
Scholastic UK Ltd., Euston House, 24 Eversholt Street, London NW1 1DB
Scholastic Ltd., Unit 89E, Lagan Road, Dublin Industrial Estate, Glasnevin, Dublin 11
Made in Jefferson City, U.S.A.     40

Twinkle, twinkle, you're a star!

Believe in yourself and you'll go far.

Up above the world so high

Dance like a diamond in the sky!

Twinkle, twinkle, share that glow!

Be true to you wherever you go.

Twinkle, twinkle, you're my friend.

Beam out boldly until the end.

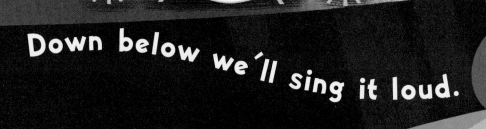

Down below we'll sing it loud.

Let your voice shine, sing it proud.

Twinkle, twinkle, be the light!

Use your shine to make things right.

Twinkle, twinkle, start that spark.

Brighten up the deepest dark.

Ups or downs: Have no fear.

Friends will always be right here.

Twinkle, twinkle, you're a star . . .

**ALWAYS** believe in who you are.